To Jacob
(MTAY)

Table of Contents

STICK CAT

By tom Watson

Two Cats and a Baby

SCHOLASTIC INC.

ISBN 978-1-338-54785-6

12 11 10 9 8 7 6 5 4 3 2 1   19 20 21 22 23 24

Printed in the U.S.A.   40

First Scholastic printing, January 2019

Typography by Jeff Shake

Chapter 1A

IT'S MARY'S BIRTHDAY

You know Mary, right?

I wrote the first Stick Cat story for her.

And the second.

And the third.

MARY

She's in my class.
And she's, umm,
you know, cute.

There I said it.

She's also obsessed with cats. She has two

pet cats, but that's not all. She also has cat sweaters, bags, notebooks, pencil erasers, and loads of other cat stuff too. For real.

In English class, I usually write Stick Dog stories. But I got Mary to, you know, like me or whatever, by writing Stick Cat stories and letting her read them. She even asked me to the Sweetheart Dance. And I'm pretty sure that she was super-impressed with my dancing skills. I got rhythm, you know what I mean?

And guess who has a birthday next month?

That's right, Mary.

And guess what I'm going to give her?

Right again.

Another Stick Cat story.

Note to self: tear out this chapter before giving to Mary.

Chapter 1

BEAUTY SLEEP

It was morning and the sun began to rise above the big city.

Edith was half asleep on the windowsill. Her eyelids drooped down to nearly shut. Stick Cat jumped up softly and quietly next to her.

Nobody in their apartment—not Stick Cat, Edith, Goose, Tiffany, or Mildred—had gotten much sleep the previous night.

Who is Mildred?

Good question.

A lot has happened since the last Stick Cat story when he and Edith captured the dangerous and fearsome burglar named Tuna Todd.

I'll try to catch you up real quick-like.

Okay, after the police took Tuna Todd away, Goose (Stick Cat's roommate) and Tiffany (Edith's roommate) saw each other for the first time through the hole in the wall between their two apartments. Edith and Stick Cat had scratched and clawed at the wall to make that hole so they could spend their days together when Goose and Tiffany went to work.

Well, when Goose and Tiffany saw each other through that hole, two totally important things happened.

First, they fell in love at first sight.

GOOSE   TIFFANY

Second, when it was obvious that love was in the air, Edith said, "Gross."

Edith doesn't like romance.

What else happened? Let me tell you.

After dating a few months and taking a trip to Paris, France, Goose and Tiffany got married back in his hometown, which is a few hours outside of the big city. It was a lovely day. In the evening at Picasso Park, there was a wedding celebration with fireworks. And there was a buffet that included barbecue ribs and mashed potatoes. There was also a huge, tall, elegant, multitiered wedding cake.

Edith, umm, ate a LOT of that cake.

And Stick Cat shared an entire layer of that wonderful cake with five hungry stray dogs. There was a poodle, a dachshund, a Dalmatian, and a couple of others. You might have read all about that in my story *Stick Dog Crashes a Party.*

When they arrived back in the big city, Tiffany and Edith moved into Goose and Stick Cat's apartment.

About ten months later, Mildred was born.

That's who Mildred is. She's the baby. Everybody just calls her Millie.

Millie is not a very good sleeper.

She likes to wake up in the middle of the night. And when she wakes up in the middle of the night, Millie likes to cry.

This is fine with almost everybody in the apartment. That's because they know that Millie is just a baby. They know that she gets hungry. She wants to know where she is. She might be afraid of the dark. She might be lonely.

Everybody is fine with it.

Well, almost everybody.

Goose is fine with it.

Tiffany is fine with it.

Stick Cat is fine with it.

Edith, however, is not fine with it.

"Did you hear that little beast last night?" asked Edith when Stick Cat hopped up next to her on the windowsill.

"You mean Millie?"

MILLIE?

"Of course I mean Millie," Edith huffed. Her frustration showed. "I mean, that tiny monster just would not shush up!"

"I think babies often wake up in the night like that," Stick Cat commented. He had heard these complaints from Edith before. And he was more interested, frankly, in watching the sunrise. This was Stick Cat's favorite part of the day. He was just beginning to eyeball the different sections of the city as the sunlight crept across the rooftops. He watched as the windows went from a dull, flat gray to a glistening gold and orange when the sunlight reached them.

He didn't watch for long though.

Edith demanded his attention.

"Stick Cat, look at me," she said.

Stick Cat looked at her.

"I don't think you're taking this problem seriously enough," Edith said. Her eyes were fierce-looking.

"What problem?" Stick Cat asked. Truthfully, he had already forgotten what Edith was talking about.

"The not-sleeping problem!"

"Oh," Stick Cat replied. "I don't think we should worry about it. I think most babies have trouble sleeping. Millie will probably grow out of it soon. She'll be fine."

"Stick Cat!" Edith exclaimed. There was the tiniest hint of anger in her voice. "I'm not talking about Millie's sleeping problem. I'm talking about *my* sleeping problem!"

"Oh."

"If I don't get a good eighteen or twenty hours of sleep every day, it can affect my mood," Edith explained.

"A lack of sleep can affect your mood?"

"Most definitely."

"How so?"

"Well, I can become selfish, obstinate, prissy, and overbearing, that's how," answered Edith. "Instead of my usual caring, wholesome, kind, and patient self."

Stick Cat hesitated a single second before responding, "I see."

I SEE.

Edith seemed content that Stick Cat understood now. She repositioned herself a bit on the windowsill, swishing her tail from one side of her body to the other. She did it with just a touch of flair, allowing the very tip of her tail to snap a bit before fluttering down to stillness. She grinned to herself at her own magnificence before continuing the conversation.

"So?" she asked.

Stick Cat asked, "So what?"

"So, how are we going to stop this rotten munchkin from crying in the middle of the night?" Edith asked. She seemed exasperated that Stick Cat was not following her train of thought this morning.

"I'm not sure there's anything we can do," Stick Cat replied honestly.

"Well, I don't want to hear it," huffed Edith. "There must be something we can do about this itty-bitty menace to society."

"I think babies just cry sometimes," Stick Cat said, and turned from Edith and stared out the window. He was just starting to feel the change in temperature outside—just feeling the day's first hint of warmth as the sun's light began to wash across the city.

"I have an idea," Edith said.

Stick Cat turned back to her. "What is it?"

"Well, you know how I'm a most excellent singer, right?"

Now, Stick Cat knew that Edith was definitely NOT a most excellent singer. In fact, her piercing, screeching, earsplitting "singing" reminded him of someone rubbing sandpaper across some violin strings while a fire alarm was blaring.

But Stick Cat didn't mention this.

Instead, he said, "Yes."

"So, maybe I should put my finely tuned harmonies to work on Millie when she wakes up at night."

"How so?"

"I could sing her a lullaby," Edith said with pride. "She would fall right back to sleep with my magnificent melodies. I would single-handedly turn Screaming Demon Millie into Sleeping Angel Millie. I'd be a hero!"

This was, without a doubt, the absolute worst idea Stick Cat had ever heard. If Edith suddenly started "singing" in the middle of the night, the whole building—heck, the whole big city—would wake up and be scared out of their wits. But he, of course, couldn't say that to Edith.

"Umm," Stick Cat said as he worked to find something to say.

And while he delayed, Edith tapped her left front paw on the windowsill three times.

Tap. Tap. Tap.

TAP-TAP-TAP

She wanted a response.

But Stick Cat didn't need to provide one, thank goodness.

Because right then Tiffany called out, "Breakfast time!"

Edith jumped down from the window and raced toward the kitchen.

BREAKFAST TIME!

Chapter 2

THE MISSING SAUSAGE LINKS

Stick Cat hurried to the kitchen too. Nowadays, he looked forward to his meals almost as much as Edith.

You see, when Tiffany and Edith moved in, Stick Cat's meals got WAY better. Goose had always provided Stick Cat with pouch food. He would switch the flavors every couple of weeks, but Stick Cat's food always, always, always came from a plastic pouch.

BORING CAT FOOD

Not anymore.

Tiffany had been making hearty gourmet meals for Edith for years. And now that they all lived together that meant Stick Cat got gourmet meals too.

Today's breakfast was huevos rancheros and sausage links.

Edith was already eating when Stick Cat arrived. His bowl was right next to hers.

"How are the eggs?" asked Stick Cat.

"Good," Edith mumbled as she chewed. After swallowing, she added, "Tiffany put more salsa in mine. Extra spicy. I like my eggs extra spicy!"

"I know you do," Stick Cat responded, and smiled. Edith was always happy around mealtime.

"Because *I'm* extra spicy."

"I know you are," Stick Cat, still smiling, said. He looked down into his bowl. "And how is this sausage link?"

"They were really good."

"'They'?" asked Stick Cat. "Did you get more than one sausage link?"

"Yes, we both got three," Edith answered,

and dropped her head toward her remaining eggs.

Stick Cat looked into his bowl again. There was a small mound of eggs with a little salsa on top and there was one sausage link.

One sausage link.

One.

Exactly.

It only took a few seconds for Stick Cat to develop a theory about what had happened to his other two sausages.

"Umm, Edith?"

She answered in a mumble through a

mouthful of spicy—extra spicy—scrambled eggs and salsa. "Mm-hmm?"

"Do you know what might have happened to my other two sausage links?"

What occurred next was quite revealing— and provided Stick Cat with an obvious answer.

Edith, who before Stick Cat's question was

munching and chewing and swallowing furiously, suddenly stopped. The fur on the back of her neck shot up. She had gone from being a busy, hungry cat one second to a totally still and busted cat one second later.

Stick Cat saw this and grinned to himself. He didn't really care about the two sausage links. But he did like to have fun with Edith about such things.

"Edith?"

"Yes?" She still hadn't moved.

Stick Cat repeated his question. "Do you know what happened to my sausage links?"

Edith finally relaxed. The fur on the back of

her neck collapsed back down to its normal position. She inhaled and exhaled more comfortably. Her shoulders became less stiff. To Stick Cat, it appeared she had come up with an answer.

"Are you sure you haven't eaten them already?" she asked.

"I just got here."

"Hmm," Edith said. "It is a curious thing, isn't it?"

Stick Cat did not respond. He looked forward to Edith's next theory. In a few seconds he heard it.

"Maybe they jumped over to my bowl," she posed.

"Can sausages jump?"

"I don't see why not," Edith said. There was a glimmer of hope in her voice, as if she believed that Stick Cat might actually be buying into her notion. "They are warm and chewy. Kind of springy. Maybe they hopped over here. Maybe."

"It's possible, I guess," said Stick Cat. "If so, could you pass them back, please?"

"They aren't over here," Edith said. "They must have just kept hopping and jumping— those crazy little buggers! They must have jumped from your bowl and then just continued hopping. I bet they jumped right out of the kitchen window. Crazy, right? They must be long gone."

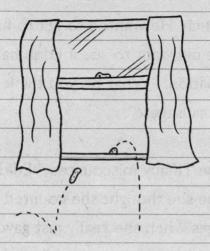

"Edith?"

"Yes?"

"The window is closed."

"Oh," she said, and paused. "Maybe they didn't jump at all."

"If I haven't eaten them already and they didn't jump out of the kitchen window," Stick Cat said. He wasn't going to prolong this too much. He wanted to get to his breakfast. But he did want to see if Edith had another explanation. "What do you think happened to my sausages?"

"Maybe Tiffany miscounted," Edith suggested. "Maybe she thought she counted three sausages when she really just gave you one."

"You think she miscounted to three?"

8, 5, 1, 6, 2...

"It's possible," Edith said. Then she whispered, "She's not all that bright."

"I think she can count to three."

"Well, then," Edith said. She had tired of the conversation. "I give up. I guess your missing sausages will remain a mystery forever."

Stick Cat watched as Edith, apparently convinced that the conversation was now complete, leaned down to lap some water. He smiled at her.

"Edith?"

"Yes," she answered between drinks.

"I think your hopping sausages idea might be right, after all."

"You do?"

"Yes, I do," answered Stick Cat. "I think my sausages hopped out of my bowl just like you said."

"I'm glad you can see the logic-ocity and smart-issiness of my sausage-hopping theory," Edith said. She seemed delighted that Stick Cat had come around to actually believing one of her explanations.

Seeing this, Stick Cat decided to offer Edith a ready-made excuse. And he decided it was time to eat his breakfast.

"I think those gosh-darn sausages hopped right into your mouth," he said. "It's not your fault you ate them."

"I think I would have noticed if your sausages sprang into my mouth, Stick Cat," Edith said slowly. She had the strangest look about her right then. Her head tilted just a tad to the left, her pupils dilated, getting bigger and bigger. Her whiskers twitched. She didn't look quite devious, but she did look menacing. She was not going to take the blame. Edith had thought of another idea.

Stick Cat couldn't tell what she was up to. He lowered his head to take his first breakfast bite.

"Wait a minute, wait a minute," Edith said. She had finished her meal and had more time to talk now. "I know what happened. I know who took your scrumptious sausages!"

Stick Cat swallowed his first bite and lifted his head from his bowl. He asked, "Who?"

"Millie!" Edith said. "That sneaky, chubby

villain must have crawled over here earlier. I
bet *she* did it!"

"Edith," Stick Cat said. "Millie doesn't know
how to crawl yet. She can roll over, lie on
her back, and sit up. That's it. She needs to
be carried everywhere."

"Maybe she started crawling when nobody
was looking, Stick Cat!" Edith shot back.
"Did you ever think of that?"

"No," he answered. "I hadn't thought that

she started crawling and you, me, Goose and Tiffany never noticed. Even though, you know, if she did, she'd be crawling all over the place. And I think it's a pretty big deal—like a really big deal—when a baby starts to crawl."

"Maybe she doesn't want anybody to know so she can sneak around and cause trouble—like stealing sausages," Edith explained. You could tell she liked this idea of blaming Millie for something. "That would be just like her."

 Stick Cat didn't believe any of it, of course. But that didn't stop Edith from continuing.

"That's it, all right! Mystery solved," Edith

summed up. "That malicious, marauding Millie rolled over from her back, crawled right over here, and took your sausages! Then she crawled right back to wherever she was, rolled over onto her back again, and ate them!"

Edith looked at Stick Cat, smiled, and nodded. She was very happy with her explanation. It got herself off the hook while simultaneously shifting the blame to Millie, who had interrupted so much of her beauty sleep last night.

"I doubt that Millie—" he started to say, but he didn't finish.

"I'm sure of it," Edith interrupted. "Imagine—just imagine—what that rotten, twisted munchkin has done in the past several hours! First, she robs me of my precious slumber time. Then she robs you of your tasty, smoky, chewy sausages! That sniveling, sniffling sneak!"

"Well, I'm not quite sure that—" Stick Cat began to say in Millie's defense.

But he was interrupted again.

This time, he was interrupted by the doorbell.

Chapter 3

GRANDMA COBB

It was Grandma Cobb, Tiffany's mom.

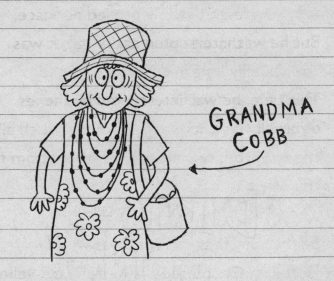

GRANDMA COBB

When the bell rang, Tiffany hurried to the door to let her in. "Mom!" she exclaimed, and gave her a big hug.

Ever since Edith was a kitten, she had known Grandma Cobb.

Grandma Cobb looked like she always did. She wore a lovely, flowing, long flower-print dress. She wore a big floppy hat, carried an oversized shoulder bag, and wore a very long purple-and-yellow beaded necklace. She wore that necklace every day. It was really, really long and Grandma Cobb looped it around her neck several times. When it was unclasped, it could stretch all the way from one side of the living room to the other.

Edith's very first memory was when Grandma Cobb used that purple-and-yellow necklace to play with her. Grandma dangled it in front of Edith—and Edith batted at it with her little kitten paws. Grandma

swished the necklace across the floor and
Edith bounded after it with all her kitten
energy. Grandma looped it
loosely around Edith's neck
to play dress-up—and Edith
pranced in front of the
mirror with all the
kitten prissiness she
could muster.

Edith adored Grandma Cobb. She
remembered when Grandma would pick
her up and bring her close. She would
stare into her eyes and say, "You can be my
grandkitty."

As soon as she saw Grandma Cobb enter
the apartment, Edith hustled toward the
door in several joyous leaps and bounds. She
rubbed her left side against Grandma's right
leg.

"There's my grandkitty," she said, leaning down and stroking Edith gently across the top of her head.

Edith purred deeply.

Stick Cat moved across the living room too, but not as fast as Edith. When he arrived, he asked, "Are you happy to see Grandma Cobb?"

"Happy?! I'm elated! Overjoyed!" Edith exclaimed. She purred and rubbed against Grandma constantly as she spoke. "She's the best! The absolute best!"

"I've heard you mention her before," Stick Cat said. He had only seen Grandma Cobb once or twice before. "I can tell how much you like her. Why is that?"

"Grandma recognizes my unique and
charming personality traits," Edith answered,
still purring away. "She always tells me how
pretty I am. She admires my magnificent
tail. She brings me treats and presents. She's
amazing!"

"Well, I'm glad—" Stick Cat started to say.

"Look!" Edith interrupted, and pointed
up at Grandma who was
now digging around in that
huge shoulder bag to fetch
something. "She's getting
me a present or a treat
right now! I'm sure of it!"

Stick Cat watched as Grandma searched
inside that big bag with her left hand.

"There it is."

She pulled out a small plastic object with a circle on the end. It rattled.

Upon seeing it, Edith propped herself up  on Grandma's leg and stared longingly at that plastic object.

"No, not for you," Grandma said, looking down at Edith briefly. She then looked up and across the living room. "Where's my granddaughter? Where's my Millie?"

That's when Goose came in from the kitchen. He was holding Millie in his arms.

"There she is!" Grandma exclaimed, and hurried over. Edith fell off her leg. "There's the most beautiful girl in the world! Look how big! Four months already!"

Stick Cat saw the look of disappointment on Edith's face. It lasted for only a split second.

"I brought this for you!" Grandma said, and shook the rattle before handing it to Millie. Millie took it eagerly and immediately began to chew on it.

Again, Edith looked disappointed. But, again, that look lasted just a single moment.

"There's probably something in the bag for you too," Stick Cat reassured Edith. "It's a big bag."

"I'm sure you're right," Edith said confidently. "It's Grandma Cobb, after all. And I'm her grandkitty."

It was precisely that moment when Grandma said something that made Edith even more confident.

"Who wants to see my necklace?" she said loudly and playfully.

"Told you!" Edith screeched, and pivoted quickly. She leaped away from Stick Cat at the apartment's door and toward Grandma in the center of the living room. In midair, Edith exclaimed, "I *love* that necklace!"

After two more leaps, Edith landed at Grandma's feet. She looked up and saw her swinging that purple-and-yellow necklace in the air. The colorful beads twirled and sparkled as they caught the sunlight streaming through the window.

Edith got up on her hind legs and propped herself against Grandma again.

But Grandma didn't even notice.

She was too busy watching Millie reach, grab, and grasp that necklace with her fingers. Edith saw this and dropped back to all fours on the living-room carpet.

By this time, Stick Cat had worked his way to the middle of the living room too. He saw the sadness on Edith's face.

"Don't worry about it," Stick Cat said, trying to comfort Edith. "It's just because Millie is new."

The look of disappointment lasted slightly longer than the previous one. But, again, her love of—and faith in—Grandma Cobb were far too strong and sturdy to leave any trace of lingering doubt.

And something else occurred right then that increased her confidence.

Tiffany said, "We're leaving now, Mom."

Edith snapped her head quickly in Stick Cat's direction. "Did you hear that?" she asked with pure happiness in her voice.

"I did," he answered. He wasn't quite sure

why Edith was so gleeful.

"Everybody is leaving!" exclaimed Edith. "I get Grandma all to myself!"

Then Tiffany said something else that changed Edith's mood quickly.

"Are you sure you'll be okay here by yourself with Millie?"

"Of course," Grandma said. She held Millie up in the air and smiled at her. "This isn't my first time with a baby, you know. I did raise you and your two brothers, Tiff. I'll take good care of her while you're gone. Don't worry about a thing."

"Okay, okay," Tiffany said.

"We'll be absolutely fine, right?" Grandma

asked Millie. Millie giggled.

Edith had, of course, heard this entire conversation—and understood exactly what it meant.

"Wait a minute," she said, turning back to Stick Cat. Her gleeful and confident attitude had suddenly turned to doubt and anxiety. "They're not taking Millie?!"

Stick Cat answered honestly, "I don't think so."

"Millie is *staying here*?!"

"I believe so."

"With me and Grandma?!"

"I think that's right."

"But I can't compete with that chubby little cherub!"

Stick Cat took a single moment then to consider his response. He had never seen Edith like this before. Edith was many things. She was prissy, funny, spoiled, and brave. Her bravery wasn't always well-placed. She tended to do dangerous things often without thinking about them—she thought parachuting or hitching a ride with a couple of pigeons were excellent ways to cross the alley from up on the twenty-third floor, for instance. Edith was, in all respects, an absolutely confident cat. She was totally confident in her appearance, her ideas, and her actions. She was even infinitely proud of her own singing abilities—even though Stick Cat and anyone else in a five-mile radius knew how terrible her ear-ringing shrieking was.

No. Stick Cat knew this about Edith for sure: she did not lack confidence.

Ever.

But now, facing Millie in a competition for Grandma's attention, Edith suddenly seemed to doubt her own chances.

"Edith," Stick Cat said. He was ready to give her self-esteem a boost. "As soon as Millie takes a nap, I'm sure Grandma will remember what a charming, gorgeous, playful companion you are."

CHARMING.
GORGEOUS.
PLAYFUL.

Edith pulled her mouth to one side for a few seconds then, thinking about Stick Cat's words.

"Well," she said after a pause to think about them. "I don't think I need Millie to fall asleep for me to defeat her in a battle for Grandma's affections. Given a level playing field, I think I can handle just about anything."

"I believe that's true," Stick Cat responded. He was pleased to see Edith's confidence at least partially restored.

"And you certainly did sum up my traits nicely," Edith added. "Charming, gorgeous, and playful are some of my most endearing attributes."

"Indeed."

"Especially gorgeous."

"Especially."

"Would you like to add anything else?" Edith asked.

ANYTHING ELSE?

"Anything else what?"

"Any additional characteristics about me?"
Edith asked. "You know, flesh out your
description about me. Add a few details."

Stick Cat squeezed his lips together, smiled,
and then said, "You're elegant. You're fluffy.
You're magnificent."

"All true," Edith said, and nodded.

She also waited.

She wanted to hear some more.

To encourage Stick Cat, Edith provided a

prompt. "What about my singing voice?"

"Umm," Stick Cat said. It seemed like he was trying to find the right words to use. He found them. "You sing like nobody else I have ever heard before."

Edith liked the sound of that.

"Would you like me to sing something for you right now?" she asked, and cleared her throat quickly. Without waiting for Stick Cat's reply, Edith inhaled and began to let out a high-pitched, off-key, scratchy, screaming screech.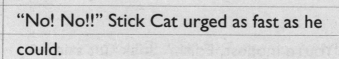

"No! No!!" Stick Cat urged as fast as he could.

Edith stopped.

"Why not?"

"Umm," Stick Cat said. "Umm. If you begin
to share your amazing musical talents,
Goose and Tiffany will probably want to
stay and rejoice in your concert. Then
you won't get to have that alone time with
Grandma."

"Good point," Edith said, almost fully
satisfied. "Anything else? You know,
about me?"

Stick Cat, utterly relieved that Edith was not
going to sing, was happy to provide her with
another compliment.

"You're modest, Edith," Stick Cat said.

"You're quite modest."

"Modest?" Edith asked. "What's that mean?"

"It means you're not full of yourself," Stick Cat began to explain. "You don't brag. You have confidence in yourself, but you don't have to show everybody that you're confident in yourself."

"That's true," Edith said, and nodded her understanding. "I am *totally* modest. I am the most modest cat—the most modest anything—on the entire planet. Nobody is more modest than me. I'm the best at modest! The absolute best!! Why, you can't even mention the word 'modest' without envisioning me and all my beautiful modesty. Nobody can out-modest the lovely and vivacious Edith! Nobody anywhere. Nobody anytime. Edith, Edith, Edith! Modest, modest, modest! That's me, all right!"

Stick Cat smiled and simply said, "That's you, Edith. That's definitely you."

While this conversation happened, Tiffany and Goose put on their jackets and paced to the apartment's door.

"You two go on and have a nice time," Grandma called to them as they opened the door. "Don't worry about a thing."

"Okay, Mom," Tiffany said. "You can give Millie a little applesauce straightaway. She might be hungry."

"I'll do that right now," Grandma answered, turned on her left heel, and carried Millie into the kitchen.

Just as Goose and Tiffany exited the apartment, Goose asked, "Should we warn her about the bathroom door?"

Tiffany answered, "No. We'll only be gone for a few hours. Besides, the knob is just loose, not broken."

Goose said, "Okay."

The apartment door squeezed shut.

Stick Cat did not know it at the time, but he would wish later that Goose and Tiffany *had* warned Grandma Cobb about the damaged bathroom doorknob.

It would have made things a lot less complicated.

And a lot less scary.

Chapter 4

LEFTOVERS

Grandma Cobb was in the kitchen with Millie—and Edith took no time getting in there too. She sprinted in that direction as soon as the door squeezed shut behind Goose and Tiffany.

It made perfectly good sense to Stick Cat that Edith wanted to get to the kitchen as quickly as possible. Her favorite person— Grandma—was in there. And her favorite thing—food—was in there too.

In the few seconds it took for Stick Cat to enter the kitchen, Edith had already

positioned herself in the folds of Grandma's flower-print dress. Stick Cat saw a familiar look on Edith's face.
Her chin was lifted in the air, her eyes were open wide, and her eyelids fluttered precociously.

"Here comes the first bite!" Grandma said excitedly.

"I'm ready!" Edith said, and stretched upward toward Grandma.

But Grandma, as you probably know, was not going to feed that first bite to Edith, of course.

She was going to feed it to Millie.

Grandma knew it.

Millie knew it.

Stick Cat knew it.

Edith did *not* know it.

"Edith," Stick Cat said, coming close.
"I think Grandma is feeding Millie."

"Don't be ridiculous," Edith replied. She
did not change her position at all. In fact,
she stretched upward a little farther. "She
may have given that plastic rattle-y thing
to Millie. And she may have played with
that necklace with Millie. But I refuse to
believe that Grandma Cobb came to the
kitchen to feed *her* instead of *me*. I'm her
grandkitty!"

"But Millie is in her high chair," Stick Cat said kindly. "That's where Millie sits when she gets fed."

"*I'm* the grandkitty!" Edith reiterated.

"Goose and Tiffany just said Grandma could give her some applesauce."

"I'm *the* grandkitty!"

"She's not even looking at you."

"I'm the *grandkitty*!"

Stick Cat gave up.

But Edith did not.

Each time Grandma dipped that small silver spoon into the applesauce jar, Edith stretched a little higher. Each time, Edith truly believed the next bite was for her. And each time, Grandma gave it to Millie.

It took fifteen spoonfuls to finish the jar. And Stick Cat watched Edith's face and expression the entire time.

It started with joy.

Then hope.

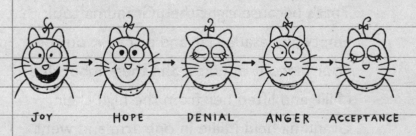

JOY HOPE DENIAL ANGER ACCEPTANCE

Then denial.

Then anger.

Then acceptance.

Edith dropped down to all fours. She turned to Stick Cat and whispered a single, simple thing.

"I think Grandma likes that pudgy pip-squeak more than me," she said quietly. "She's forgotten about me entirely."

"It's okay, Edith. Let's go—" Stick Cat began to say. He didn't finish.

That's because right then Grandma took that empty applesauce jar and placed it on the floor in front of Edith. She then unbuckled Millie and lifted her from the high chair. Grandma held Millie in one arm and went to the sink to rinse off the spoon and wash Millie's face.

"Look!" Stick Cat exclaimed. "She didn't forget about you at all!"

Edith looked down into the empty jar and asked, "What am I supposed to do with this?"

"You can lick the inside of the jar!" Stick Cat said. He did his best to sound excited, but he could tell Edith was not at all enthusiastic about this prospect. "You can lick the rim!"

"Lick the rim?!" Edith asked.

"Yes!" Stick Cat said. He really tried his best. "Around the rim is the best part! I bet Grandma saved it just for you!"

Edith wasn't buying it.

She turned from the applesauce jar and toward Stick Cat.

She asked, "Do you know what this is?"

"It's applesauce," Stick Cat answered. "Tasty, tasty applesauce. Just for you! From Grandma! For her grandkitty!"

"This," Edith said, and nodded her head in disgust at the jar. "This is leftovers. Millie ate it first."

Stick Cat didn't say anything then.

Edith made a single—and final declaration. "I *DON'T* eat leftovers."

And then Edith huffed out of the kitchen. Stick Cat followed her into the living room. He had never seen her so upset. Edith jumped onto the blue couch and curled up in a corner of it.

"What are you doing?" asked Stick Cat after propping himself up with his front paws.

"I'm taking a nap, that's what."

"Would you like to do something else instead?"

"Like what?"

"We could play Treasure Hunt or StareDown," Stick Cat suggested. He wanted to do something to lift his best friend's mood. "We could get one of Goose's sock

67

balls and bat it back and forth for a while.
That would be fun!"

Edith shook her head
and closed her eyes.

Stick Cat lowered himself back to all fours
on the floor. He was about to head to the
windowsill to gaze out at the big city while
Edith slept.

But he didn't get the opportunity.

That's because right then Grandma came
into the room with Millie in one arm and a
blanket in the other.

And that's when everything changed.

Chapter 5

CLUNK!

Grandma put Millie down on a pink blanket on the floor in front of the couch.

"Now I'm going to use the bathroom," Grandma said to Millie. "I'm going to leave you here for just a minute or two."

Millie cooed and babbled some sounds in response.

BABBLE!
BABBLE!
BABBLE!

Edith sighed and opened her eyes. The
nearby activity had disturbed her—and
distracted her from falling asleep. She asked,
"What does a girl have to do to get some
sleep around here?"

"Grandma is just going to use the
bathroom," Stick Cat said. "She'll be back to
take care of Millie in a minute."

"I know you're not going to go anywhere,"
Grandma said, and folded the soft pink
blanket over Millie partway. "You haven't
even started crawling yet. So I know you're
safe here."

Before leaving for the bathroom, Grandma tickled Millie under the chin for a few seconds.

Millie giggled and then looked up from the floor at Edith on the couch. Millie gurgled some noises at her.

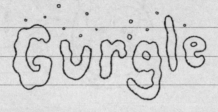

"I think Millie is trying to talk to you," Stick Cat suggested.

"Is that so?" Edith replied, and sighed. She didn't seem very interested.

"It sure looks like it," Stick Cat said. "She can't take her eyes off you."

This comment, however, seemed to make

an immediate—and huge—impression on Edith. Of all the things in the world, Edith liked being admired the most. She gave Millie a smile of encouragement and asked, "What do you think she's saying?"

"I bet she's complimenting you about how smooth and shiny your fur looks today."

Edith examined herself for a few seconds, then said, "She certainly has fine taste and exceptional skills of observation, I'll give her that."

"She definitely does," Stick Cat said, and then crossed the living room and hopped up to the windowsill. It was cracked open a couple of inches. That was just how he liked it. He enjoyed feeling that cool city breeze move through his fur. It was calm and quiet then for a single minute.

A single minute.

Then Stick Cat heard two separate and distinct noises inside the apartment.

First, the toilet flushed in the bathroom.

Then *CLUNK!*

That was the second sound.

Stick Cat snapped his head in the direction of that second sound. He wanted to know what made that noise.

On the floor in front of the bathroom door was one thing.

The doorknob.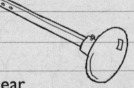

And Stick Cat could hear Grandma yell something from inside the bathroom.

"Oh no!"

Chapter 6

TRAPPED

Stick Cat leaped from the windowsill and hurried to the bathroom. When he got there, he pawed at the doorknob and examined it. He looked up to see a hole in the door where the knob used to be.

By scooting away from the door, he could just see through that hole into the bathroom.

What he saw was Grandma's eye looking right back at him.

Then her eye disappeared.

A few seconds later, the door shook and shimmied.

He heard Grandma grunt as she pushed against it four times.

It didn't budge.

It was stuck.

She was stuck.

Inside.

And Stick Cat, Edith, and Millie were on the outside.

Grandma's eye came back to the hole. It was wide—and it was panicked.

"The doorknob broke!" she exclaimed. "I can't get the door to move at all. I don't know what to do!"

Stick Cat moved to the door and propped up against it. By stretching as high as he could, Stick Cat could just see through that hole. Grandma pushed an index finger through the hole and petted his cheek the best she could.

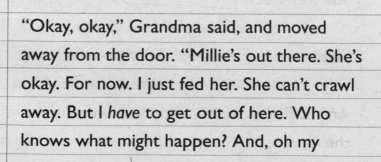

"Okay, okay," Grandma said, and moved away from the door. "Millie's out there. She's okay. For now. I just fed her. She can't crawl away. But I *have* to get out of here. Who knows what might happen? And, oh my

goodness, Tiffany and Goose will never let
me babysit again. Think, Carol, think!"

Stick Cat heard her move around inside the
bathroom. He heard her open and close the
sink cabinet drawers and doors. She pulled
the shower curtain to one side, exposing the
window, and then back again. She opened
and closed the mirrored cabinet above
the sink. She searched for something—
anything—she could use to open the door.

Stick Cat hurried to the living room.

Edith was on her belly, leaning off the front
edge of the couch. She stared down at Millie
on the floor.

"Edith! Edith!!" Stick Cat exclaimed as he got there. He jumped up on the couch next to her. "We've got big, big trouble!"

"Shh, Stick Cat," Edith said quickly. "I'm talking with Millie."

This caught Stick Cat completely off guard.

"You're what?"

"I'm talking with Millie."

Now, even though Stick Cat had an emergency on his paws, he just had to investigate this a bit further.

He asked, "You can understand what Millie is saying?"

"Of course," Edith replied. "I'm super-smart. I have a very good brain. I know exactly what she's saying."

"What's she saying right now?"

"She just asked me how I get my eyelashes to curl and flutter so exquisitely. It's girl-talk, Stick Cat. It's no wonder you can't understand her like I can."

While Edith described her new baby-interpreting skill to Stick Cat, Millie was completely content lying on her back on the floor. She was gurgling and sticking her fingers in her mouth.

"I see. Thanks for explaining," Stick Cat said,

and smiled. Only Edith, he thought, could figure out a way to make Millie's baby noises into compliments for Edith. And he was delighted that she seemed to be warming up to Millie. He turned to more pressing matters. "Grandma is trapped in the bathroom. The doorknob broke!"

"Grandma? What Grandma?" Edith asked. She didn't seem to care at all. "Grandma who?"

WHAT GRANDMA?

"Grandma Cobb, of course."

"Oh, right. Her," Edith said slowly. She did not quite have disgust in her tone of voice.

But she did have disdain. She was still upset and now considered Grandma unworthy of her attention. "I remember her. She's the one who did not have a toy in her bag for me, did not play with her necklace with me, and gave me leftover—*leftover*—applesauce to eat. Yes, yes. I remember her, all right. I remember her quite clearly."

"She's your favorite person," Stick Cat reminded.

"No," Edith said, and shook her head. "Millie is my favorite person now. You should hear all the wonderful things she's saying about me."

Stick Cat understood that Edith was upset with Grandma. But he didn't have time to navigate her hurt feelings right now. He knew that taking care of Millie was a big and important job. And he knew that babies were fragile and could be hurt easily. And he knew that Grandma was desperate—absolutely desperate—to get out of that bathroom and back to Millie.

Stick Cat had to help her do that.

He just didn't know how.

"Edith," he said. "I know you're upset with Grandma right now, but I was wondering if you might have any ideas about how we could get her out of the bathroom?"

Edith was absolutely silent then. She said

nothing for more than a minute. She looked back and forth between Stick Cat on the couch and Millie on the floor. Millie was getting louder, gurgling and babbling more and more.

"Edith?" Stick Cat asked again. "Any ideas?"

"I tell you what," Edith finally said. "If you'll just leave me and Millie alone, I'll help you get Grandma out of the bathroom."

"Deal," Stick Cat said. "How do I do it?"

"It's easy."

"It is?"

"Totally."

"What is it?"

"You pull her through that hole where the doorknob was."

"Excuse me?"

"You pull her through the hole."

"Umm," Stick Cat said, and paused. "I think she's a little too big to fit through that hole."

"Well, I don't mean you pull her through right *now*," Edith said, and shook her head. "You pull her through later."

"Later?"

"That's right."

"Later when?"

"After she's lost enough weight and can fit through the hole."

Stick Cat pulled his mouth to one side. He contemplated his words a moment before speaking. "It's a terrific idea, Edith. It really is. But she would need to lose almost every single pound."

"So?"

"So," Stick Cat said. "That's not possible."

"Well, that's not my problem. That's *her* problem," Edith replied, and stood up to all fours. She hopped off the couch. "I'm going to get that rattle for Millie. She just told me she wants to play."

Stick Cat jumped off the couch too. He headed to the bathroom to help Grandma.

When he got there, something unusual was sticking out of that hole in the door.

Something very unusual.

Chapter 7

MILLIE DOESN'T MESS AROUND

The wooden handle of the toilet plunger was sticking out of that hole. It poked in and out. It jiggled left and right. It wiggled up and down.

"Come on, come on," Grandma said from inside the bathroom as she moved the handle in every possible direction. Stick Cat was at the door now and could hear her clearly.

He knew that toilet plunger. It had been in the bathroom cabinet for years. He had seen it every day that he and Edith had met through the hole in the wall. That hole was all boarded up now though.

He wanted Grandma to know he was there. He wanted her to know he hadn't forgotten about her—and that he wanted to help.

He just didn't know *how* to help.

Yet.

He meowed.

As soon as he made that noise, Grandma pulled the toilet plunger handle out of the door and into the bathroom.

She looked through the hole.

And saw Stick Cat.

"I see you there," she said. "I thought maybe I could knock something inside the door or the lock. Maybe shake something loose. It didn't work."

Stick Cat meowed again.

"I don't know what to do," Grandma continued. It sounded like she was talking to herself more than Stick Cat—like she was hoping an escape plan would come to mind if she spoke out loud. "There's no phone in here, obviously. There's nothing. A sink. A tub. A shower curtain. A window. A toilet. Nothing I can use. Nothing."

Stick Cat could not see Grandma through the hole anymore. She had stood up. He could hear her pacing about on the other side of the door—looking all around for anything to use.

"I have to get back to Millie," Grandma said. "I'm not strong enough to knock the door down. I'd break my shoulder on my first attempt. I can't—"

Grandma didn't finish her sentence.

She was interrupted.

By Millie.

Millie started to cry in the living room.

Now, there's something you need to know about Millie.

She was cute and playful and sweet, like all babies are. But when Millie decided that it was, indeed, time to cry—Millie didn't mess around.

She didn't start with a little whine. She didn't groan or sigh. She didn't start at a low volume and build up slowly to get louder and louder until she reached her highest volume.

No.

When it came to crying, Millie's approach was as loud as possible.

And as fast as possible.

"WAAAAAAAAAAAHHHH!"

"Oh no!" Grandma exclaimed. She stooped down to the hole and looked out. She couldn't see into the living room, of course. She called, "It's okay, Millie. It's okay, Millie. Oh, what am I going to do?!"

Stick Cat pivoted and raced off to the living room to try to help. When he got there, he couldn't believe what he saw.

Chapter 8

EDITH SHAKES

Edith had succeeded in finding the rattle. She had brought it to Millie.

She showed it to Millie.

She rattled it for Millie.

It was, umm, the *way* Edith showed it and rattled it for Millie that was so alarming.

Edith leaned back on her rear haunches right next to Millie, who was still lying on her back on the pink blanket. Edith held

the rattle in her front paws right above Millie's face.

And when I say right above Millie's face, I mean, like, *right* above Millie's face.

Like three inches above her face.

Maybe two inches.

And Edith shook that rattle as fast and as furiously as she could.

"Look at the rattle! Look at the rattle, Millie!" Edith screamed. Her eyes were wide open. "Isn't it fun?!"

LOOK AT THE RATTLE!

Millie obviously didn't like this kind of playing at all.

Stick Cat bounded over to the scene.

Edith turned her head calmly to him when Stick Cat arrived next to her.

"I don't think she likes this rattle toy," Edith said. As she spoke, Edith continued to shake the rattle vigorously right above Millie's face. "No matter how hard I shake this thing, she isn't having any fun. I got it real close so she can see it. But she doesn't like it at all. Why do you think that is?"

UMMM...

"Umm, I have no idea," Stick Cat said. He had to think for a moment. He needed to get the rattle away from Edith. She was scaring the living daylights out of Millie rather than playing with her. Edith didn't recognize this, of course. She didn't *know* she was scaring Millie, but she was scaring her just the same. "Speaking of ideas, your first Grandma-rescue plan was so great I wonder if you could come up with another one for me?"

"Of course I can," Edith replied, appreciating the compliment. She still shook the rattle. "I've thought of another plan already."

"Great," Stick Cat said as fast as he could. "Before you tell me, maybe you could hand me that rattle. It's so loud—and I want to be able to hear your plan clearly."

To Stick Cat's great
relief, Edith stopped
shaking it and handed
it to him. Immediately,
Millie stopped wailing and screaming. Edith
didn't seem to notice.

Stick Cat put the rattle down on the floor.

"All right," Edith said. "Since you think it will
take too long for Grandma to lose enough
weight to fit through that hole, I have
another idea."

"Super. What is it?"

"She uses the toilet."

"Umm," Stick Cat responded slowly.
"What?"

"The toilet. She uses the toilet."

"Okay," Stick Cat said. He had a couple of emergencies on his paws. Grandma was trapped in the bathroom and completely desperate to get back to Millie. Millie was settling down, but still whimpering. She had, after all, just been scared out of her wits by Edith. He wanted to deal with these two situations as effectively—and as quickly— as he could. And Stick Cat suspected that Edith's toilet plan—whatever it was—would not be helpful. He asked quickly, "How do we use the toilet to get Grandma out of the bathroom?"

Edith sighed. "Do I really have to explain it? It's perfectly obvious."

"Please do."

"Okay," Edith said, and inhaled deeply. "First, Grandma steps into the toilet and stands there. Then—"

"Wait, wait," Stick Cat said. "I'm sorry to interrupt, Edith. But did you say that Grandma should stand in the toilet?"

"That's exactly what I said," she confirmed calmly. "Was that difficult to understand or something? I mean, really, Stick Cat, try to keep up."

"Okay, I will," he answered. "It's just that I've never thought of people standing in toilets."

"Don't worry about it, Stick Cat," Edith replied. It sort of sounded like she was bragging a little bit. "I'm the one doing the thinking here. That's pretty obvious. And pretty typical."

"Okay, then," Stick Cat said, and smiled a bit to himself. Edith didn't see him. He said, "So, Grandma stands in the toilet. What happens next? How does she get out of the bathroom?"

"She flushes the toilet."

"She flushes it?"

"She flushes it."

"Umm," Stick Cat said, and paused. "Why?"

"Well, so she goes down the toilet, of course," Edith explained. Her whole Grandma-rescue plan appeared perfectly reasonable, logical, and simple to her.

"Okay. She goes down the toilet," Stick Cat said. He figured it was probably better—and quicker—to just accept Edith's strategy than to ask a bunch more questions about it.

"Then she spins around in the water for a few seconds," Edith continued. "You know how the water swirls around right when you flush the toilet?"

FLUSH!

"It does?" Stick Cat asked. "I didn't know that. I've never noticed. I've never actually looked into a toilet before."

"Oh, I have," Edith said. "Right when you push the silver handle, there's a big WHOOOOOOSH! of water, then it all spins around real fast like a mini-tornado, then SKLUUUURPSH! the mini-tornado gets sucked out real fast-like. It's totally awesome!"

Stick Cat was curious about something, you could tell. His face was scrunched up slightly and his left eyebrow was lifted a bit. He knew he had to rescue Grandma, but he just had to ask Edith something.

"How did you learn so much about flushing toilets?" he asked.

"I've flushed them before," Edith answered matter-of-factly. "Quite a few times."

"Why?"

"Oh, whenever Tiffany gives me some little gift that I don't like, I'll often flush it down the toilet," Edith said. "It sends a pretty clear signal to her about my particular likes and dislikes."

"I see," Stick Cat said. "I guess I do remember you telling me about flushing some pink booties that you didn't like."

"That's right," Edith said. "Tiffany knitted them for me a few winters ago. It took her weeks and weeks. She's not a very skilled knitter, to be honest. Not that crafty."

"I forget. Why didn't you like them?"

"They were pink and it was winter," Edith explained. She seemed to enjoy Stick Cat's interest in the subject. "I don't wear pink in the winter. That's more of a spring color."

"Right, right," Stick Cat said.

"I've flushed other things than those booties though."

"You have?"

"Most definitely," said Edith. "Ribbons, bows, things like that. She gave me a truly disgusting ribbon last year that I flushed immediately."

"Why didn't you like it?"

"It was purple."

"You don't like the color purple?"

"I *adore* the color purple," Edith said. "But purple things demand glitter and sparkle. Purple things need to be adorned and decorated with little silver and gold highlights. This specific ribbon was just flat and dull. No sparkle whatsoever."

"It sounds, umm, terrible," Stick Cat said. "Just terrible."

"It was hideous."

"So you flushed it."

"Yes indeed," said Edith. "I gave it the old flush-a-roo!"

Stick Cat decided then to hear the rest of Edith's plan. He still hadn't figured out how to help Grandma escape from the bathroom. He began to ask, "So, after Grandma flushes herself, what—"

But, apparently, Edith had more to say.

She interjected, "I also flush food."

"What?!"

"Food," Edith repeated. "I also flush food."

"Why?"

"Tiffany is not exactly a master chef or anything," Edith explained. "If she doesn't prepare something that meets the needs of my sophisticated palate, down it goes. Flush-a-rama!"

"What food have you flushed?"

"A couple of years ago, I flushed an entire portion of fettucine Alfredo."

"Why?"

"I could tell that Tiffany had made that cheesy white sauce with milk and margarine instead of cream and butter," Edith said, and shook her head at the memory. "The real texture and complexity of the dish was lacking."

"I understand," Stick Cat said—even though he didn't understand any of this. He could never act in such ways. But he really needed to keep this moving. "So, after Grandma flushes herself, what happens?"

"She shoots down the toilet and swooshes down all the pipes in our building," Edith continued. "As she travels down twenty-three floors to street level, she's swimming, floating, and frolicking in the water. She's having the best time. It's like a vacation at the beach! Except she's not at the beach, she's in some pipes. And there's no sun, it's totally dark. And it's not wide-open space with other people, it's more like really tight in those pipes and she's alone. But, otherwise, exactly the same."

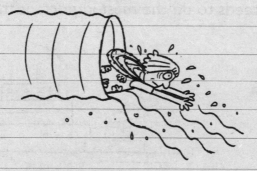

"Right, yes. Exactly the same," Stick Cat said slowly.

"Eventually, she shoots out of the pipes and into the river," Edith continued without pause. "Playfully avoiding the river traffic—

you know, tugboats, barges, sailboats, humongous navy destroyers, and aircraft carriers, those kinds of things—she swims to shore. I envision her doing the backstroke and spraying a spout of water high up into the air. Arriving refreshed and relaxed on the riverbank, Grandma walks to our building and takes the elevator up here to the twenty-third floor. She lets herself in and proceeds to do the *most* important thing."

"Pick Millie up and make sure she's okay?"

"No, Stick Cat," Edith said. "I said the *most* important thing."

"Isn't helping Millie the most important thing?" Stick Cat asked.

"Not at all."

"What is?"

"Well, flushing herself, swimming down through the pipes, avoiding boat traffic, climbing the shore, walking to our building, and taking the elevator will require a good bit of time," Edith explained. "By the time she gets here, it will be early afternoon. And you know what early afternoon is, don't you?"

"What?"

"It's my lunchtime, that's what!"

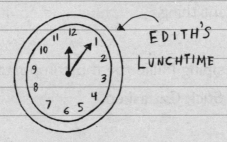

EDITH'S LUNCHTIME

"So, instead of ensuring that Millie is safe and happy, Grandma is going to come in and fix your lunch?"

"I assume so," answered Edith. "It doesn't need to be anything fancy, mind you. Some grilled tuna with a peppercorn demi-glace perhaps. Or a simple slice of beef tenderloin with a red-wine reduction. Perhaps a swordfish steak with a mango and red pepper chutney."

"So, umm, something simple."

"Right. Something simple."

Stick Cat nodded his head. He didn't say anything because, truthfully, he could think of absolutely nothing to say.

This actually worked out perfectly.

That's because right then Grandma started *bang*ing against the bathroom door.

Chapter 9

EDITH TRIES AGAIN

BANG!

"I have to get back to the bathroom, Edith!" exclaimed Stick Cat. He was terribly afraid that Grandma was going to hurt herself. She was, after all, quite old and frail. And that door was heavy, solid wood—and absolutely stuck. Stick Cat was sure that if she rammed into it over and over, then Grandma might break some bones—or even worse.

He took three fast, long steps toward the bathroom, gaining speed rapidly with each paw-fall.

"Wait, Stick Cat!" Edith called.

He stopped as suddenly as he had started.

"What is it?" he asked, snapping his head over his shoulder to look back at Edith. "What can I do for you?"

"I gave you a plan, remember?" Edith asked.

"I remember," Stick Cat said. "Your plan was for Grandma to flush herself down the toilet. How could I possibly forget?"

"I know," Edith acknowledged proudly. "Brilliant, right?"

"Umm, totally."

"Well?"

"Well, what?" Stick Cat asked.

BANG!

"I gave you a genius plan to help Grandma escape from the bathroom," Edith explained. "And now I'm a bit worried that Millie might cry again—and I don't want her to do that. She is my new favorite person, after all. Maybe you could give me a plan to keep her from crying."

"Okay," Stick Cat said. He took a step toward them. He certainly didn't want Edith shaking that rattle so menacingly at Millie's face again. He thought of something quickly.

"Maybe she's cold. I think babies like to be nice and cozy. Maybe you could make her warmer," Stick Cat said fast. He looked at Millie lying on that soft pink blanket on the living-room floor. There was plenty of extra blanket on either side of her.

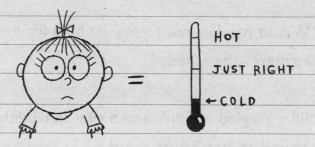

Stick Cat lifted one edge of that extra blanket and allowed it to fall gently over Millie. Immediately, Millie curled and tucked

herself into the soft,
warm folds of that extra
material. She liked it, you
could tell. She grew a
little more quiet.

"Not a bad idea," Edith said, noticing how
Millie had calmed a bit. "Let me just ask her."

Edith leaned down toward Millie as Stick Cat
watched.

"Would you like me to make you a little
warmer?" she asked.

Millie gurgled at Edith and a tiny spit-bubble
popped on her lips as she did.

Stick Cat felt a little ridiculous asking, but he
asked anyway. "What did she say?"

"First, she mentioned that she really loved the blue bow I'm wearing today," responded Edith. "Millie said it brings out the blue in my eyes. She said my eyes remind her of brilliant blue sapphires. Then Millie said, yes, she would greatly appreciate me making her warmer."

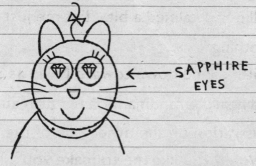

SAPPHIRE
EYES

Stick Cat smiled and said, "Great!"

Then he sprinted to the bathroom.

Right when he got there, Grandma Cobb threw her weight against the jammed door once more.

BANG!

It didn't move an inch.

Or a half of an inch.

Or a quarter of an inch.

Nothing.

He heard Grandma moan in pain and sigh in frustration on the other side of the door.

Stick Cat meowed as loud as he could to get her attention. He looked through that doorknob hole and was relieved when, after several seconds, Grandma stooped down and looked back at him. At least she had stopped smashing into the door for the time being.

"I see you there," Grandma said as she looked through that hole. "I heard you over there too. Did you come to check on me? Did I scare you with those big banging noises? I'm sorry if I did."

Stick Cat purred loudly.

"It's almost as if you understand me," Grandma said. She seemed slightly surprised at the thought of that. She stood up and away from the hole, but kept talking. "I can't stay crouched down like that for too long.

It hurts my back. And now both my shoulders hurt too. I want to get out of here so badly. I'd do anything."

Stick Cat purred again. He wanted Grandma to know he was still listening—and that he was trying to figure it out.

"I heard Millie cry a few minutes ago. It kills me to hear a baby cry," she continued. Her voice started to quiver and crack. Stick Cat couldn't tell, but he thought Grandma might be starting to cry herself. "And when it's my granddaughter— my only grandchild— that feeling is worse. Way worse. And when I can't do anything about it, it's the worst thing in the whole world."

Stick Cat purred loudly again.

But he wasn't sure if Grandma could hear him anymore.

Millie had started to cry again.

"What's happening in there?!" Stick Cat whispered to himself, and yanked his head around to look into the living room—to look at Edith and Millie. When he did—and what he saw—made Stick Cat forget about Grandma entirely.

Stick Cat turned and sprang forward. He landed and raced away from the bathroom and toward Edith and Millie. As he sprinted, Stick Cat observed what Edith was doing to try to make Millie warm.

And he understood why she had begun to cry.

Edith paced slowly in a counterclockwise circle around Millie. Her neck was stretched downward and her head hovered just a couple of inches over Millie's body and head as she circled.

Edith was blowing on Millie.

She was taking great, deep, gasping inhales of air and then exhaling in sudden, powerful bursts. As she circled, Edith blew those huge gusts on different parts of Millie.

She blew on her shoulders and continued to circle slowly.

She blew on her tummy and circled.

She blew on her knees.

Her feet.

Then up and around to Millie's other side.

She blew on her knees again.

Then her tummy.

Her shoulders.

And then—much to Stick Cat's great anguish—on Millie's head.

When Edith hovered there midstride, she took a deep breath, held it in, and then let it out with humongous force across Millie's face.

WHOOOOOSH!

He saw Millie's mouth squeeze shut in a grimace.

He saw Millie's hair blow back from her forehead.

He saw Millie's eyes squeeze tightly shut.

And he heard Millie cry even louder.

He bounded the rest of the way to them.
When he got there, Stick Cat was happy
that he got Edith's immediate attention.
She stopped circling and blowing. She
straightened up and looked at him.

As calmly as he could muster, Stick Cat
asked, "Edith, what are you doing?"

"I'm trying to make her warm. Just like you
suggested—and just like she asked for,"
Edith explained simply. "But let me tell you

something, Mr. Man-With-a-Plan, this idea of yours is a real stinker. No good at all."

"I'm sorry," Stick Cat said quickly. He had noticed that Millie had already quieted and calmed down some now that Edith wasn't, you know, stalking, hovering, and blowing on her. "What happened?"

"Well, I covered her with some more blanket—and she got more quiet. Not all the way or anything. She was still gurgling and babbling. She made some truly adorable comments about my tail. She admired its fluffy texture and swishing qualities. This girl really knows what she's talking about."

"What happened next?"

"Well, I got to thinking," explained Edith. "And as you know, Stick Cat, I'm one of the world's great thinkers. I'm, like, really smart."

"Yes, umm, I know."

"I was thinking," Edith repeated. "If covering her with some blanket quieted her down a little bit, then making her even warmer would quiet her down a lot."

"And?"

"And I thought blowing some hot air on her might just do the trick."

"So you, umm, circled her and blew on her as hard as you could?"

"Yes."

"And as close as you could?" Stick Cat asked.

"That's right," Edith answered. "Who wouldn't want to have the sweet-smelling warmth of my own breath breeze across them?"

"I see," Stick Cat said. He wanted to change the subject—and he knew just how to do it. "So, Millie was admiring your tail. Is that right?"

"What's not to admire?" Edith asked in loving reference to her own tail.

"It's quite puffy," Stick Cat complimented.

"I really think my tail is more fluffy than

puffy," she corrected.

"Your *fluffy* tail," Stick Cat amended.

Edith nodded and smiled. She said, "My tail truly is magnificent and fluffy, isn't it?"

"Yes," he answered, exhaled, and smiled. "It is."

Edith turned around to face away from Stick Cat. She turned her head over her shoulder and stared at her backside. Edith swished her tail in a smooth, graceful arc. She allowed it to settle to the floor with a final flick.

"Look at it," she sighed. "Just look at it."

Stick Cat got the feeling that he would need

to watch—and pay homage to—Edith's tail
for a while.

But that was not the case.

Because right then something came falling
out of that hole in the bathroom door again.

It wasn't a two-pound grandma who could
now suddenly fit through the hole.

It wasn't the wooden handle of the toilet
plunger.

It was something else entirely.

Chapter 10

MARASCHINO CHERRIES

It was Grandma Cobb's long purple-and-yellow necklace.

"Here, kitty!"
Grandma called.
"Here, kitty, kitty!"

"I'll be right back," Stick Cat said, and hustled back to the bathroom.

Grandma Cobb's necklace was extremely long. When she wore it, the necklace wrapped around her neck several times. It hung in five long loops all the way down to her stomach. Stick Cat could tell just how

long that necklace was when he arrived
outside the stuck bathroom door.

It was bunched in a big loose pile at the foot
of the door.

And it was still falling out.

And Grandma called
again, "Here, kitty,
kitty! Here, kitty!"

Stick Cat meowed to
let her know he was
there.

"Oh, good! I can hear you," Grandma said
from the other side of the door. "I'm glad
you came. Just let me get the rest of this
pushed through."

After fifteen or twenty more seconds, the end of the purple-and-yellow necklace fell out of the doorknob hole and landed with a jangle and *CLINK*. Grandma Cobb's eye peeped out from the other side immediately.

"There you are!" she exclaimed upon spotting Stick Cat. "I'm happy you're here. I heard Millie crying before. Oh, it just bothers me so, so much that I can't get to her! And then I thought, what would I do if she was crying? And I remembered she loves this necklace of mine. And maybe—just maybe—you would be so smart and take it to her. Maybe it will keep her busy if she gets upset again."

Stick Cat purred. He knew it was a good idea. He had seen Millie's fascination with the necklace earlier.

He picked up one end of the necklace with his mouth.

"You *are* a smart kitty!" Grandma said happily.

You could tell instantly that she felt a little better knowing that she could help Millie in this way. Stick Cat could hear the joy in her voice. He hurried off to the living room, dragging the purple-and-yellow necklace behind.

"Go, kitty, go!" yelled Grandma.

When he got back to the living room, Edith was smiling at Millie.

"Do you know what her cute, chubby little cheeks remind me of, Stick Cat?"

"No, what?" asked Stick Cat after dropping the necklace.

"Maraschino cherries."

"What are maraschino cherries?" Stick Cat asked.

"You've never heard of maraschino cherries?" Edith asked. She seemed quite surprised.

"No."

"I'm astonished!"

"What are they?" Stick Cat asked again.

"Maraschino cherries go on top of an ice cream sundae, of course," Edith answered.

"I know what ice cream is. I've seen Goose eat it before," said Stick Cat. "But what's a sundae?"

"Let me tell you," Edith said. Stick Cat could tell she was getting excited. Edith liked to talk about food. "An ice cream sundae is a sweet and delectable dessert. Tiffany gives me a sundae on my birthday! It's three scoops of ice cream—vanilla, chocolate, and strawberry. Then, there's a huge fluffy layer of whipped cream over that. A warm caramel sauce is then delicately drizzled atop the whipped cream. A smattering and scattering of chopped salty nuts—I prefer finely minced cashews, but almonds or hazelnuts will do in a pinch—goes on top of that. Then finally the maraschino cherry goes on the very tip-top."

"And that's the best part?" asked Stick Cat.

"Maraschino cherries are most certainly the very best part," Edith answered, and continued. "It's like a regular cherry that has been supercharged with sugar and thick sweetened syrup. It's the most brilliant, bright, and unnatural red in the world. But that's not the best part about a maraschino cherry!"

"It's not?"

"No!"

"What's the best part?"

"It's *when* you eat it!" Edith explained.

"When do you eat it?"

"You eat it at the very end!" Edith
exclaimed. She was so excited. It was as
if she was reliving the ecstasy of every ice
cream sundae she had ever consumed.
"The very end!"

"Why do you eat it at the very end?"

"Because it's the ultimate reward!" Edith
said excitedly. "Don't you see? At the very
beginning that cherry is floating on top
of the sundae. But as you eat the other
parts—the ice cream, the whipped cream,
the caramel sauce, and the finely chopped
nuts—the maraschino cherry slowly
descends through the distinct and delicious
flavor layers. It gathers and accumulates

each separate flavor on its glorious journey to the bottom of the bowl. By the time you've finished all the other ingredients, the cherry has made its slow, scrumptious plummet to its ultimate destination!"

Edith paused, sighed, and licked her lips before continuing.

"Throughout its travels," she went on, "it's picked up a whole collection of traveling companions. A few nutty morsels have come along for the ride. Some supple caramel sauce has joined the trip, attaching itself to the cherry's bright red rind. Drippy drops of sweet whipped cream surround the cherry in a delicate, seductive goo. And then finally—finally, finally—the cherry flutters to its final stop at the bottom of the bowl through a liquid-y melt of vanilla, chocolate, and strawberry ice cream. Then—and only then—is it time for that final bite!"

"The cherry?" asked Stick Cat.

"Not just any cherry," Edith replied.
"Oh no, sir. The ultimate cherry!"

"The ultimate cherry?"

"The ultimate cherry!"
Edith gushed. "It's a sweet, syrupy cherry
covered in whipped cream, caramel sauce,
chopped nuts, and vanilla, chocolate,
and strawberry ice cream. It is a sweet,
delicious treat that is *covered* in sweet,
delicious treats!"

"Maraschino cherries sound delightful—and
delicious," said Stick Cat.

"They are," answered Edith. She licked her

lips some more. "They most certainly are."

"And I'm glad Millie's bright red cheeks reminded you of them," Stick Cat added.

"Me too!" Edith exclaimed.

Stick Cat turned around. He picked up the purple-and-yellow necklace. He pulled a bunch of it nearer and close to Edith.

"Look what I brought," he said to Edith.

"Grandma's necklace?" Edith asked suspiciously. You could tell that her feelings were still hurt. She remembered that Grandma Cobb had entertained Millie—not Edith—with that necklace earlier. "How did you get it?"

"She pushed it through the doorknob hole a few minutes ago. And I went to get it," he explained. He did not like to make things up, but Stick Cat thought it was important to add, "I'm pretty sure she wanted you to have it."

"Really?" Edith asked. There was a hint of doubt in her voice.

"She said, umm, she felt bad about not paying enough attention to her grandkitty."

"What else did she say?" asked Edith.

"Umm," Stick Cat said as he thought quickly. "She said that maybe you would like to play with the necklace. And that, umm, she knew it was one of your favorite things."

"Really?" Edith asked.

"Really," Stick Cat said.

Edith grinned and said,
"Good old Grandma."

Stick Cat was happy to hear absolute
forgiveness in Edith's voice.

Edith picked up the necklace lovingly
between her paws. It clinked and jingled. Its
purple-and-yellow glass beads reflected and
sparkled in the living room's bright ceiling
light. The strong metal chain that connected
the beads glistened too.

Edith felt better.

And so did Millie. She was watching,

listening, and settling down—as fascinated
with that clinking, sparkling necklace as
Edith was.

"Good old Grandma," Edith whispered
again.

"Grandma," Stick Cat said. "She's still stuck
in the bathroom. How am I going to get
her out?"

"Don't worry about it, Stick Cat," Edith
pronounced as she played with the necklace.
"I know how to get her out."

"You do?"

"I do."

"Excellent," Stick Cat said. "Let's hear it."

Chapter 11

GIANT BALLOONS

"My plan all starts with Christmas," Edith said without hesitation.

"Christmas?"

"Christmas," confirmed Edith.

"But Christmas is months away."

"That's right," Edith said. Apparently, this fact didn't bother her or hamper her potential Grandma-rescuing strategy at all. Edith was still dangling, fidgeting, and rattling the necklace. And much to Stick Cat's pleasure, Millie was still focused on it.

"So, what's your plan? How does it involve Christmas?"

"Well, you know what happens at Christmas, right?"

"Santa comes?"

"No."

"We put up a tree?"

"That's not it."

"We hang stockings?"

"Not even close."

"We open presents?"

"Wrong, wrong, wrong," Edith said. "Before all of those things. What happens?"

"I don't know, Edith," Stick Cat said. He really wanted to keep this moving along. "What happens before all of those things?"

"The Thanksgiving Day Parade, of course," Edith answered. "That's the real start of the Christmas season."

"Okay," Stick Cat said slowly. He didn't see

how the big annual holiday parade through
the city could have any connection to
rescuing Grandma from the bathroom.
"How does your plan involve the parade?"

"Don't you know?"

"No. No, I don't."

Edith shook her head. She seemed surprised
that Stick Cat didn't know how the
Thanksgiving Day Parade months from now
could help rescue Grandma Cobb from the
bathroom today. "I guess I'll just have to tell
you then."

"Please do."

"Well, what's the most important thing
about the parade?" Edith asked.

"The marching bands?"

"No."

"The colorful floats?"

"Try again."

"The big crowds of people?"

"Give it another shot."

"Santa Claus at the end?"

"Wrong again," Edith said, and sighed. "You

are really not giving very good answers today, Stick Cat."

He inhaled deeply, exhaled slowly, and said, "Maybe you should just tell me, Edith. I can't wait any longer. I always enjoy hearing about your plans so much."

"It's the balloons!" exclaimed Edith. "The giant balloons!"

Stick Cat knew what Edith was talking about. He had watched the parade in late November every year since he and Goose had moved to the big city. Interspersed among the slow-moving floats and the loud, rhythmic marching bands were

giant helium-filled balloons of every
possible shape. There were huge inflatable
cartoon characters, Christmas trees, and
superheroes. The balloons bobbed and
floated all along the parade's route through
the city. And Stick Cat could see the great
balloons float down the street at the end of
the alley. Some of them floated even higher
than he was on the twenty-third floor.

So he knew what Edith was talking
about. He just didn't know how the giant
Thanksgiving Day Parade balloons would
help Grandma get out of the bathroom.

"Okay," Stick Cat said again. "I know what
those balloons are. They're really awesome.
But how do they help Grandma? What's
your actual plan?"

"Easy," Edith said. "Grandma opens the

bathroom window and climbs out on the ledge. Then when she sees one of those balloons floating by, she leaps off the ledge and lands on it. Then she jumps to a lower balloon and a lower one and so on and so on. Until she reaches the street. Then she walks to our building and comes on up."

"I understand," Stick Cat said slowly, and nodded his head. He didn't think Edith's plan made any sense, of course, but he did understand it.

Edith added, "And then she comes in and fixes my lunch."

"Oh, right," Stick Cat acknowledged. "I forgot that the first thing she'll do upon her arrival is fix your lunch."

"That's correct," Edith said. "So, to get started, all Grandma needs to do is open the bathroom window and stand outside on the ledge. Easy-peasy, pumpkin pie."

"Wait a minute," Stick Cat said, and stood perfectly still. "Wait a minute."

"What is it, Stick Cat?"

"What did you just say?" he asked, still completely motionless.

"Easy-peasy, pumpkin pie?"

"No, before that," Stick Cat said. His eyes had a glazed faraway look in them. "How does your plan start?"

"Grandma stands out on the bathroom window ledge."

"That's it!" Stick Cat exclaimed, and  bounded to the living-room window. When he got there, he hopped to the sill and pushed the window up.

"Stick Cat, what are you doing?"

"I know how to save Grandma!" Stick Cat
yelled. "You did it again, Edith!"

Edith shrugged her shoulders and said just
one thing.

"Well, of course I did. I'm Edith."

Chapter 12

WHERE'S EDITH?

Stick Cat pushed the window up, leaned his head out, and saw the bathroom window ledge about three feet away. He thought he could jump to it.

He and Edith had, after all, jumped the other direction to old Mrs. O'Mahoney's kitchen window ledge once. That was even farther than the bathroom window ledge. That was a couple of years ago when they saved Mr. Music after he got stuck in a big black grand piano.

Stick Cat looked down to the alley.

Twenty-three floors down to the alley.

His vision became instantly blurry. His head became instantly dizzy. And his stomach became instantly queasy. He ducked back inside.

"What are you doing, Stick Cat?"

"I was thinking," he started to say. He stopped, looked down at the carpet, and shook his head to clear it. Then he continued. "I thought I'd jump from the ledge here over to the bathroom window ledge and get Grandma's attention. I think she will let me in. It's a fairly long jump for *me*, but I think *she* might be able to just step across. It would be dangerous, but maybe there's some way we could make it safe or something."

"And my whole jumping-from-the-window-ledge-onto-a-giant-balloon-during-the-Thanksgiving-Day-Parade plan is what gave you the idea?" asked Edith.

"Yes," Stick Cat said. He had regained his steadiness and sense of equilibrium now. "Yes, it did."

"Jeez," Edith said proudly. "Sometimes I even surprise myself with my smartness."

Stick Cat smiled at that.

"But now that I've looked down to the alley and thought about it, I'm not so sure," Stick Cat said. "It's a longer jump than I thought. And we are twenty-three floors up."

Edith joined him at the window. They both propped themselves up, leaned out, and eyeballed the bathroom window ledge. Stick Cat sensed that uncomfortable feeling return to his stomach and came back inside. He dropped back to all fours and took a couple of steps toward Millie to check on her. She was holding the necklace and seemed fine for the time being.

"Yeah. The more I think about it, it's way too dangerous to even try," Stick Cat said as he turned back to the window. "Maybe we can come up with another—"

But Stick Cat didn't finish his sentence.

Edith was gone.

Chapter 13

ACTION, STICK CAT, ACTION

Stick Cat lurched to the window. He was afraid to look down—afraid to see Edith plummeting to her doom.

That's when Edith called, "It's an easy jump! It's no big deal."

She was on the bathroom window ledge.

"How did you get over there?!" Stick Cat asked. He was so happy—and astonished— to see his best friend safe, sound, and completely calm.

"What do you mean 'How did I get over here?'" Edith called back. "What do you think? Do you think I took a helicopter? Do you think I sprouted wings and flew? I jumped, of course. Duh."

"I *know* you jumped," Stick Cat said. "It's just you did it so suddenly! We're twenty-three floors up! You didn't even think about it!"

"Thinking is for shmucks," Edith said, and plopped back on her rear haunches. She allowed her tail to fall haphazardly over the ledge and began to groom her eyebrows with the back of her left paw. She was certainly quite comfortable.

"What?"

"I said thinking is for shmucks," Edith repeated. "I am a woman of action. Action, Stick Cat, action! While you mope around thinking this and thinking that, I'm moving forward. Marching on! Taking action! You think too much, Stick Cat."

WOMAN of ACTION

"Maybe I do, Edith. Maybe I do," Stick Cat said, and smiled. He liked this proud, sure, confident side of Edith. He just didn't want to see that side of her demonstrated in such a dangerous way. He looked over his shoulder to check on Millie. She was fine. She was still occupied with Grandma's necklace. As he turned back, he added, "I might be too cautious sometimes. And I might—"

Edith jumped back.

"Edith!"

"Action, Stick Cat! Action!"

"Okay, okay," Stick Cat said quickly. "I get it.
Please stop—"

Edith jumped to the bathroom window
ledge again.

"Action!" she screamed joyfully in midair.

"Edith!"

She landed securely, turned around on
that narrow ledge, and said, "Action, baby.
That's me."

"Edith!" Stick Cat screamed. "Stop jumping

back and forth!"

"Why?" she asked honestly. "It's fun!"

"Because it's, umm, my turn now," Stick
Cat responded slowly. He still didn't want
to make that jump, but he needed to get
Edith to stop. She was plenty confident,
but Stick Cat believed what she was
doing was WAY more dangerous than she
thought. "And I think Millie is missing you."

"She's missing me?!"
Edith asked. Then
she added, "Well, of
course she is."

She jumped over, climbed back through
the living-room window, and hopped down
to the carpet. Edith hurried toward Millie.
Upon her approach, she babbled some

sounds at Edith for a couple of seconds.

Stick Cat had to ask, "What did she say?"

"Millie said she saw me jump," Edith answered without hesitation. "She is amazed at my ability, agility, strength, and prowess. She added that my bravery is unmatched and my daring unparalleled. And she marvels at my combination of power and beauty."

"She said all that?"

"Yes," Edith confirmed. "She's quite the little chatterbox."

Stick Cat grinned and said, "She certainly is."

Edith tilted and pointed an ear toward Millie

when she gurgled and cooed for another two seconds.

"And now what's she saying?" Stick Cat inquired.

"She said that while you're not quite as brave, powerful, and beautiful as I am, she still thinks you'll be able to make the jump successfully."

Stick Cat nodded his head one time and climbed out on the window ledge. "I'm going to go check on Grandma."

He did not look down.

He looked across.

"Edith just did it. Twice," Stick Cat whispered to himself. "You can do it too."

Stick Cat closed his eyes.

He heard Edith's voice echoing in his head. *Action, Stick Cat. Action.*

He concentrated his energy and leaned back on his rear legs.

He opened his eyes.

He stared at his target.

And Stick Cat jumped.

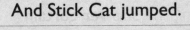

Chapter 14

FURNITURE DOESN'T WEAR JEWELRY

Stick Cat skidded a bit on the bathroom ledge's concrete surface.

And then he stopped.

He made sure of his footing and then banged on the window with his front right paw.

In just a few seconds, the shower curtain flung to one side.

There was Grandma.

Staring right at him.

It took half a second of wide-eyed surprise and recognition—and then Grandma moved very quickly.

She pulled the shower curtain completely out of the way. She stepped into the tub to better reach the window. She unlocked the window and pushed it all the way open.

Stick Cat jumped into the tub, out of the tub, and onto the firm soft footing of the mat in front of the sink.

"How did you get over here?!" Grandma asked. She was shocked. She was still standing in the tub. She looked at the open window, back at Stick Cat, and then back at the window.

Stick Cat purred.

And Grandma leaned outside. She turned her head and saw the open living-room window.

"You jumped?!" Grandma asked after ducking back inside. "Seriously?"

Despite the wonderful firm footing, Stick Cat knew he needed to communicate his idea to Grandma. He hopped up to the edge of the bathtub, up to the windowsill inside, and returned to the ledge on the outside.

Stick Cat purred and looked deliberately back and forth from one ledge to the other three times. Grandma watched him closely the whole time.

Stick Cat stepped to the edge of the ledge.

He heard Edith in his head again.

Action, Stick Cat. Action.

And Stick Cat jumped back.

He hopped into the living room, ensured that Edith and Millie were still fine, and propped himself up to the window.

Stick Cat looked at Grandma as he leaned

out the living-room window.

Grandma looked at Stick Cat as she leaned out the bathroom window.

"Do you think I could do that?" Grandma called. She looked at the distance, measuring it in her mind. "Well, I wouldn't need to jump. I think I could reach it with one big sideways step."

Then Grandma looked down.

To the alley—twenty-three floors below.

"Oh, my," she whispered. She looked across

to Stick Cat. "I don't know. I just don't know. I'm desperate to get back to Millie. And I think I can make it. I think I can. But if I slip. Oh, my."

Grandma looked down again. She reached her right arm out of the window and felt the rough creases and crevices of the brick wall with her fingertips.

"Not much to grip there. If there was just something to hold on to," she whispered. "Then I think I could do it."

"Stick Cat!"

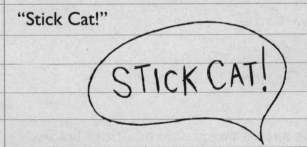

It was Edith.

He ducked back inside.

"Yes, Edith?"

"Check out what Millie can do!" Edith said excitedly.

Millie was sitting up. She gripped the necklace in her chubby little hands. Edith was a few feet away—and holding the necklace just as tightly. He could tell they were both enjoying it.

"What are you doing?"

"We're playing tug-of-war!" Edith said with

joy in her voice. "Millie the Munchkin is strong!"

Stick Cat smiled and said, "It looks like fun."

"But now we're bored," Edith admitted.

"You're bored?"

"That's right. And tired. We could both, frankly, use a long nap," Edith said. "I mean, we've played with Grandma's necklace for, like, two or three minutes. My attention span doesn't last longer than that. And neither does Millie's."

"I see."

Edith sighed and said, "A girl can only hold a necklace for so long."

Stick Cat twitched.

There was something there.

Again.

Something Edith said.

A spark.

A spark of an idea.

"What did you say?" he asked.

"I said we're bored."

"After that."

"A girl can only hold a necklace for so long."

"Hold a necklace," Stick Cat whispered to himself. "So long. A girl can hold a necklace. So long."

"Stick Cat, will you please stop repeating everything I say," Edith said. She seemed pretty bothered. "It's totally annoying."

"A girl can hold the necklace!" Stick Cat said loudly, and smiled. "It's so long. Hold the necklace!"

"Okay, okay," Edith said, clearly misinterpreting what Stick Cat was saying and thinking. She flung her end of the necklace toward him. And to copy Edith, Millie dropped the necklace too. "Don't be so demanding. You can hold it for a while. Jeez. It's not *that* great. Even Millie is bored with it now. Play with it all you want."

"I don't want to play with it, Edith!" exclaimed Stick Cat. "I want to use it to help Grandma. You gave me an idea! You did it again!"

"Stick Cat," Edith said, and lifted her chin in the air a bit. She wasn't sure what he was talking about, but she was perfectly willing to take credit for whatever it was. "You should really start coming up with your own ideas. I'm tired of solving all your problems."

"You're right," Stick Cat said quickly. He grasped the end of the necklace in his mouth and dragged it to the big blue couch. "I'll work on that."

Edith watched as he looped the end of the necklace around one of the couch's thick wooden legs.

"What are you doing?" asked Edith.

He was too busy to answer.

"Stick Cat?"

"Yes?" he replied, and looped the necklace around the couch leg a second time.

"You know furniture doesn't wear jewelry, right?" asked Edith. "I mean, that's a little silly even for you."

Stick Cat wrapped it around a third and final time.

"And you never ever use a color combination like that anyway," Edith continued. "Purple and yellow on something blue? Tacky. So tacky."

Stick Cat tied the looped necklace in a strong knot. He pulled hard on it. It was tight and secure.

He hurried to grab the necklace's other end and picked it up with his mouth. He mumbled, "I'll be right back."

He had only taken two steps toward the window when Millie started to whimper again. It looked like she might cry.

"Oh no you don't, Stick Cat," Edith said. She

then asked, "Where do you think you're going, buster?!"

OH NO YOU DON'T, STICK CAT!

"I'm going to jump over to the bathroom ledge again," he replied after dropping the necklace from his mouth. "If I can tie this other end to something in the bathroom, then Grandma will have something to hold on to when she steps across. She won't fall."

"And whose idea was it?"

Stick Cat knew how to answer that question.

"It was yours, Edith," he said. "All yours."

"And do you hear anything right now?" Edith asked. "I'll give you a hint: it starts with an *M* and ends in an 'illie.' And it sounds like she might be about to cry. I don't want her to cry."

"Umm, thanks for the hint," Stick Cat said. He focused on Millie. She made that about-to-cry sound again. "Yes, I hear Millie—and it does sound like that."

Edith asked, "What do you think I should do?"

"Millie's probably just tired and needs to sleep," Stick Cat said. "I think you just need to be patient. She will fall asleep eventually. Maybe even quickly. Can you just stay with her until I get back? Hopefully, I'll just be gone a few minutes."

"Just a few minutes?"

"Hopefully," responded Stick Cat. "And when I get back, you can go into the bedroom and take a nap and I'll stay with Millie."

"Oh, all right," Edith said. "Go on. Hustle along there. The sooner you get back, the sooner I can take a nap. Try to think of how this affects me, Stick Cat. And get a move on, for goodness' sake."

Stick Cat nodded, smiled a bit to himself, and picked up the necklace once more.

He jumped out to the ledge, pulled all of the necklace's slack, and piled it loosely on the ledge.

He peered forward.

Grandma was there leaning out of the bathroom window.

"Is that my necklace in your mouth?" she asked.

He heard Edith's voice in his head again.

Action, Stick Cat. Action.

He jumped.

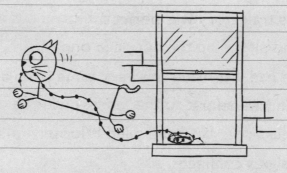

This time, Stick Cat did not land safely on the bathroom window ledge.

Chapter 15

ALMOST THERE

Stick Cat was in midair.

He soared in a graceful arc toward his destination.

His trajectory was perfect.

He had just made this very same jump a few minutes before.

He was confident.

He was almost there.

Just a few inches away.

And then the necklace, clenched in his mouth and trailing behind him, got snagged in a crack on the living-room window ledge.

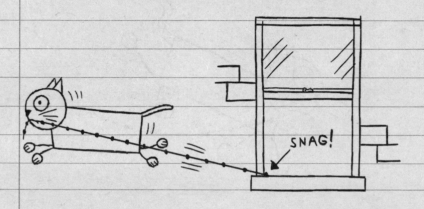

SNAG!

It jerked Stick Cat back. He knew he wouldn't make it.

He snapped his head to look down.

Twenty-three floors down.

His vision got blurry. His head got dizzy. His stomach got queasy.

And Stick Cat started to fall.

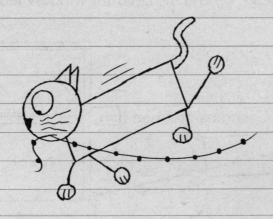

Chapter 16

A TERRIBLE SOUND

Stick Cat fell.

Until Grandma grabbed him.

She reached out from the bathroom
window, stretched even farther than the
edge of the ledge—and snatched him by the
scruff of the neck.

When Grandma snagged him from the air—

and from his plummeting doom—
the necklace jerked free from its snag and
came loose.

Grandma pulled Stick Cat through the
bathroom window, held him gently with
both arms, stepped out of the tub, and
put him down on the floor.

"What in the world are
you doing back here?"
Grandma asked. She
stroked the back of
Stick Cat's neck and
scratched him behind
his left ear—his
favorite spot.

Stick Cat purred.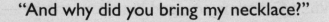

"And why did you bring my necklace?"

The jump was scary, his brief fall was frightening, and Grandma grabbing him was exhilarating. The solid footing beneath his paws made Stick Cat feel safe and sound. But Grandma's question sparked him to action.

Stick Cat looked around the bathroom, jerking his head in every direction. He needed something strong, heavy, and secure for the other end of the necklace.

"What are you looking for?" asked Grandma. "What are you up to?"

There wasn't much in the bathroom, Stick Cat realized. The tub, the toilet, the shower curtain, the cabinet, the sink.

Wait.

The toilet.

The toilet would work.

Stick Cat took the necklace, still clenched in his mouth, and wrapped it once around the base of the toilet. He had to squeeze through the space between the back of the toilet and the wall, but there was just enough room.

"What are you doing?"

He wrapped it around a second time.

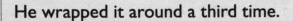

"Why are you doing that?"

He wrapped it around a third time.

"What in the world?"

Then he stopped. He could feel the tension in the necklace. It had grown tight and taut. Stick Cat pulled on it with both his paws as hard as he could and then tied a knot.

Grandma looked down at him and said, "I don't understand."

Stick Cat plucked on the necklace to demonstrate how tight and secure it was.

Grandma tilted her head a bit to the left, trying to figure out what Stick Cat was attempting to communicate.

But Stick Cat could not stay any longer.

He could provide no more hints.

That's because right then the most earsplitting, screeching, horrible sound came piercing through the bathroom window.

Stick Cat leaped to the edge of the tub and then out to the window ledge to see where that awful sound came from.

He figured it out immediately.

That terrible sound was coming from the living-room window.

And it just got worse.

Way worse.

Chapter 17

LOOK WHO'S COMING

Stick Cat could not decipher the sound.
He couldn't tell what it was. It was as
if a terrible noise was combined with a
despicable noise—and then blasted through
a megaphone.

He thought Millie and Edith might be in
trouble. He thought they might be scared.
He thought they might even be hurt.

Stick Cat did not hesitate.

He didn't wait.

He didn't think.

"Action, Stick Cat. Action," he whispered to himself.

And he leaped back to the living-room window ledge. He tumbled inside, righted himself to stand on all four paws—and saw what was happening.

Mille and Edith were not hurt.

They were not in trouble.

They were not scared.

Well, quite honestly, Millie may have been scared.

Here's what Stick Cat saw:

Edith sat back on her hind legs, had her
front paws stretched up and over her head,
and was singing—well, Edith called it singing
anyway—at the top of her lungs.

Edith's chest was puffed out. Her eyes
bulged open with pride—and from the sheer
physical force she used to project her voice
as loudly as possible.

Millie was still on her back
on that pink blanket. She
was the deepest darkest
red—almost purple—that
Stick Cat had ever seen.
Her eyes were squeezed
shut. Her little chubby
hands were clapped
tightly over her ears.

And she was wailing as loud as Stick Cat had ever, ever heard.

He waited—it seemed like forever—for Edith to pause and inhale before screeching her next earsplitting shriek.

When she did, Stick Cat screamed, "Edith!"

Thankfully, she heard him above Millie's crying and wailing.

"Oh, Stick Cat, you're back," Edith said calmly. "How's it going?"

"Umm, fine," Stick Cat answered loudly.

He still needed to speak over Millie, but he could tell that she was already calming down. Maintaining his composure, he asked politely, "What are you doing?"

"Well, while you were gone I started to think about how Millie here might just be sleepy," Edith explained. "And you said that I just had to be patient and wait for her to fall asleep."

"That's right," Stick Cat affirmed. "That is what I said."

"Well, guess what?"

"What?"

"I'm not very patient."

Stick Cat couldn't quite figure out where

Edith was going, but he did feel a bit better. His heart was not thumping and pounding so hard. His paws were on the solid floor. Millie was still crying, but not as much or as loudly as before. He just nodded at Edith.

"Yeah, I'm not very patient at all," Edith repeated. "So, I just decided to speed up the whole it's-time-for-Millie-to-go-to-sleep thing."

"And how were you doing that exactly?"

"I was singing her a lullaby."

"*That* was a lullaby?"

"Yes," Edith confirmed. "I call it, 'Twinkle, Twinkle, Little Millie.' It's an original."

Stick Cat smiled. He said, "It certainly is."

Edith liked hearing that. And she added, "It was working too."

"It was?"

"Most definitely," Edith said. "Millie was yawning and her eyes were closed. I think she was almost asleep. Then you came in and now she's crying again. But she definitely liked my singing. She has excellent taste in music."

Stick Cat figured out quickly how Edith had misinterpreted things. Millie had not been yawning, she had been wailing and screaming. But Stick Cat figured Edith couldn't hear that over her own, ahem, singing. And Millie's eyes were closed not because she was getting sleepy, but because she was trying to hide from the whole situation.

But Stick Cat didn't mention any of this to Edith.

He simply said, "I'm sorry I interrupted you."

"It's okay. My throat was starting to hurt anyway," replied Edith. She then took a big inhale of air and asked, "Would you like to hear the rest? The rest of my lullaby?"

"No, no!" Stick Cat said as fast as he could.

"Why not?"

"I don't want you to, umm, hurt your throat anymore."

This seemed reasonable enough to Edith, and she exhaled. She plopped back down to all fours. And when she did, something entirely unexpected happened. And then something happened that was even more surprising than that.

You see, when Edith dropped out of that upright singing position, her tail swooshed down—and swished around.

And her tail—that soft, fluffy tail—swished right under Millie's chin.

It tickled Millie.

She stopped crying.

Millie started to giggle.

"What was *THAT*?!" Edith exclaimed, snapping her head down to stare at Millie. "Did you hear that bizarre sound, Stick Cat?!"

"It was Millie," Stick Cat said, and smiled. He had seen the whole thing. "You made her laugh!"

"I did?"

"You did."

"How?"

"With your tail," Stick Cat explained
joyfully. "Your tail brushed beneath her
chin. It tickled her. Look, she's still smiling!"

"I can make her smile?" asked Edith. She
wasn't sure about all of this.

"You can make her smile."

"I can make her laugh?"

"You can."

"With my tail?"

"With your tail."

To test this idea, Edith positioned herself a
little closer to Millie and swooshed her tail

under her chin again.

Millie giggled even louder.

She smiled at Edith.

Edith smiled at Millie.

"She likes me, Stick Cat!" Edith exclaimed,
and tickled her some more. "She totally
likes me!"

"Of course she does. I think you're her
favorite."

"Just like she's my favorite," Edith said,

still tickling. "It makes total sense. I mean, what's not to like? I'm smart, good-looking, and charming."

"And don't forget modest."

"That's right," Edith remembered. "I'm the best in the world at being modest."

Now, Edith would have likely continued tickling Millie for some time. They were all enthralled, excited, and happy about the whole tickling thing.

But right then something caught Edith's attention from the corner of her eye.

"Hey, look," she said, and pointed at the living-room window. "Here comes Grandma."

Chapter 18

SLEEPY TIME

Stick Cat could see part of Grandma Cobb. He could see one of her feet on the window ledge and one hand clenched tightly around the necklace.

In just a few seconds, Grandma stooped
down and tumbled into the living room.

She crawled over to Millie and picked her up.

"I am never letting you go again," Grandma
whispered. There were tears in her eyes.

"Aah, some peace and quiet," Edith said,
and sighed. She didn't have the energy to
move anywhere. She curled up right where
she was near the couch, gave her shoulders

 and hips a quick shimmy to get in just the right sleeping position, and closed her eyes.

While Edith fell asleep, Grandma Cobb did several things—all while holding Millie in one arm. Millie was cooing and gurgling happily.

Grandma went to the bathroom, picked the doorknob up from the floor, and slipped it into the hole. She must have aligned it just right because when she turned it, the door clicked and opened easily. Stick Cat listened as Grandma went into the bathroom—after propping the door open with the bathroom trash can to ensure it didn't shut again. He heard the necklace jangle and clatter as she untied and unwrapped it from the toilet. He heard it fall out the window and smack softly against the wall outside. He heard the bathroom window close.

Grandma and Millie came back into the living room. She pulled her necklace inside and closed the window. After untying the other end of the necklace from the couch leg, Grandma sat down on the floor with her back against the big blue couch.

She cradled Millie in her lap—and in the folds of her flower-print dress.

She looked down at Millie, who fell fast asleep. She looked at Edith, who was asleep too. She reached out and scratched Stick Cat behind his left ear.

Stick Cat closed his eyes.

Before closing her own eyes, Grandma whispered to Stick Cat, "You're a smart kitty."

There were only two sounds in the room now.

Millie's slow, quiet, deep rhythmic breaths.

And Edith snoring softly.

After a day filled with so much loud and disconcerting noise, those two sounds brought a sense of peace and calm to the room—and lulled Grandma and Stick Cat to sleep too.

Chapter 19

KEEPING WARM

Millie woke up first.

Stick Cat heard her stir. He didn't move, but he opened his eyes to watch her.

Millie rolled off Grandma's lap and onto the floor.

Grandma didn't notice—and didn't wake up.

Millie was on her belly. She pushed herself up to her hands and knees.

Stick Cat watched as Millie crawled—
crawled for the very first time—across
the carpet toward Edith. When she got to
Edith, Millie rolled to her side right next to
her. Millie nudged her just a little, stirring
Edith enough that she opened one eye
halfway. She saw—and felt—Millie snuggle
in next to her.

Edith smirked—and then smiled. She closed
that one eye. And Edith lifted her tail—
her elegant, magnificent, fluffy tail—and
wrapped it around Millie to keep her warm.

THE END